For my son Will, who combines great imagining with excellent snacks —TS

To Willoughby and Moses —MS

Tundra Books, a division of Random House of Canada Limited, a Penguin Random House Company

Library and Archives Canada Cataloguing in Publication

Staunton, Ted, 1956-, author
Harry and Clare's amazing staycation / Ted Staunton ; illustrated
by Mika Song.
Issued in print and electronic formats.
ISBN 978-1-77049-827-3 (hardback).—ISBN 978-1-77049-828-0 (epub)
I. Song, Mika, illustrator II. Title.
PS8587.T334H37 2017   jC813'.54   C2016-900979-3
                             C2016-900980-7

Published simultaneously in the United States of America by Tundra Books of Northern New York,
a division of Random House of Canada Limited, a Penguin Random House Company

Library of Congress Control Number: 2016933059

Edited by Samantha Swenson
The art in this book was rendered in watercolor and ink.
The text was set in Bembo.
Printed and bound in China

www.penguinrandomhouse.ca

1 2 3 4 5   21 20 19 18 17

On Monday of vacation it rained.

Harry and his sister Clare stayed in and went to Mars.

Mars looked a lot like the family room, except for the volcanoes.

Harry carried the luggage. Clare, being older, carried the snacks.

Harry had an idea, but his stomach was growling and his hands were full of suitcase. "I—"

"Look out," cried Claire. "Quicksand!" She ate Harry's snack for him, since he was busy sinking.

On Tuesday, it was still raining. Luckily they could ride a Pasta Linguini racer around an indoor course in the supermarket.

Traffic was heavy. Harry wanted to turn left.

"I'm driving," said Clare.

Following a dizzying skid through the frozen food,
Clare let Harry park them in the checkout line.

"You're too little for one hand," she said. "Use two."

Harry held tight. "I—"

But it was too late. Clare was already eating their granola bars.

On Wednesday, it was *still* raining. Harry had a tough day.
About to be a dolphin at the pool . . .

. . . he was captured by a pirate queen who made him walk the plank instead.

That afternoon, while playing school, Teacher Clare sent Harry to the office for trying to eat his snack in class.

"Young man," Principal Clare warned him, "this is the fourth time this week you have been sent down to see me. I am very disappointed in you. People who eat during arithmetic are not allowed to eat at all."

Harry had an idea. "I—"

"*Quiebut!*" said the principal, whose mouth was full. "Or there will be extra homework."

When he got out of the principal's office, Harry snuck a snack up the high mountain.

In the nick of time, he heard the dreaded huffing of an
approaching Abdominal Snowman. He hid his cookies
in his pockets. He didn't share his idea, either.

At suppertime, Harry tucked away more supplies.

Luckily, nothing fell from his pockets when
he performed on the couch high-wire
trapeze trampoline, or when Lion Tamer
Clare made him jump through hoops.

On Thursday, the sun finally shone. Harry accompanied Clare on a treasure hunt through the jungle. It looked a lot like the park, except for the vines and wild animals.

"Watch out for umpire bats," whispered Clare, "and hop quietly. The hippo is sleeping." She jumped, *clunk*, over the sandbox. Harry had an idea. He kept it to himself.

"We are looking for a sunken ship guarded by a monster octopus," Clare went on. "We'd better ride our Kimono dragons so we can go faster."

Harry rode hard to keep up. He held on to his idea.

"Duck," Clare cried. "Elephant hummingbirds!" Then she reined in her Kimono dragon.
"Oh-oh. We forgot snacks. We have to go back."

Harry didn't say a word. He climbed off his dragon, took something from his pocket and began to munch.

"Is that a baby carrot?" asked Clare.

Harry didn't answer. His mouth was full.

"Where did you get that?" Clare demanded.

Harry didn't answer. He took something else
from his pocket and munched.

"Is that a cookie?" Clare asked.

Harry swallowed. "Asteroid burger," he said.

"It *is* a cookie," Clare cried. "Give me some!"

Harry said, "I have asteroid burgers. And volcano sticks."
He showed her, then nibbled. They were dry but tasty,
except for the linty bits. "Which one do you want?"

Now Clare's stomach growled. She said,
"Can I have some of both?"

"Both what?" Harry asked slowly.

"Asteroid burgers and volcano sticks,"
Clare said, even slower.

"Okay," said Harry, "I'll share. But I think the treasure is in a cave under a mountain." He held out a volcano stick.

Clare took it. "Okay. But there's still a monster octopus in the cave."

Clare and Harry climbed and dove
for hours and hours as they gathered a
magnificent collection of rare pinecone
pearls to bring home.

Harry showed Clare the prehistoric park-bench
dinosaur skeletons. Clare warned Harry about
squirrel sharks.

Riding home, Harry and Clare shared the
last of the volcano sticks and asteroid burgers.
They made a nice combination.

The mountain looked a lot like
the playground climber, except
for the monster octopus.